Turtle and Rabbit

MODERN CURRICULUM PRESS
Cleveland • Toronto

Turtle and Rabbit

Valjean McLenighan
Illustrated by Vernon McKissack

Text copyright © 1981 by Valjean McLenighan. Illustrations and cover design copyright © 1981 by Modern Curriculum Press, Inc. Original illustrations and cover design copyright © 1981 by Follett Publishing Company. All rights reserved. Printed in the United States of America. This book or parts thereof may not be reproduced in any form or mechanically stored in any retrieval system without written permission of the publisher.

Library of Congress Cataloging in Publication Data

McLenighan, Valjean.
 Turtle and rabbit.

 SUMMARY: Turtle challenges her boastful friend Rabbit to a race along First Street in this modern adaptation of the well-known fable.
 [1. Fables. 2. Animals—Fiction] I. McKissack, Vernon. II. Title.
 PZ8.2.M22Tu   398.2'452 [E]   80-13792
 ISBN 0-8136-5586-2 (Paperback)
 ISBN 0-8136-5086-0 (Hardbound)

  3 4 5 6 7 8 9 10   90 89 88

Library of Congress Catalog Number: 80-13792

Turtle and Rabbit were friends.
They did a lot of things together.

They always shared the Sunday papers.

Rabbit came over one morning.
Turtle had on some new things.

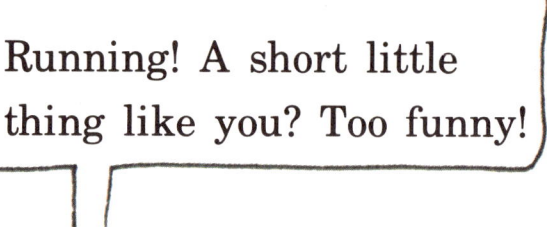

And the race was on.

Rabbit was big.
And she was fast.
At first she ran
rings around Turtle.

Rabbit danced around her friend.
For a time she ran on her hands.

Turtle kept right on going.

After a time, Rabbit got tired.
But she did not want Turtle to know.

Turtle knew what was going on.
She knew her friend pretty well.

Rabbit went right to sleep.

Turtle kept running the race.
She was slow.
But she was sure.

Fourth Street came and went.
Then there was Third Street.
Good-bye, Second Street.
Hello, First Street.

Rabbit got up at last.
But she was too late.

Turtle was there when Rabbit pulled up.

Turtle and Rabbit uses the 155 words listed below.

a	dinner	just	Peter	then
after	do	kept	please	there
all	down	knew	pretty	these
always	ever	know	pulled	they
am	fast(est)	last	Rabbit	thing(s)
and	feet	late	race	think
Animal	fine	legs	right	Third
are	first	let's	rings	this
around	for	like(d)	run(ning)	through
at	found	little	save	time
back	Fourth	long	saw	tired
be	friend(s)	look	Second	to
best	fun	lot	see	together
better	funny(ies)	make	shared	too
big(gest)	gets	maybe	she	Turtle
blues	girl	me	short	up
both	go(ing)	mean	show	want
bring	good-bye	morning	sit	was
brother	got	my	size	we
but	grandmothers	new	sleep	well
buy(s, ing)	great	no	slow	went
by	had	not	so	were
came	hands	of	some	what('s)
can	have	oh	sorry	when
cannot	hello	on	story	where
care	her	one	Street	who
Club	home	or	Sunday	why
come	House	out	sure	will
could	how	over	taking	yes
danced	I	papers	that	you
did	it	park	the	your